Cooperation

101 DALMATIANS

Adapted by Lisa Harkrader
Illustrated by the Disney Storybook Artists

Published by Louis Weber, C.E.O.
Publications International, Ltd.
7373 North Cicero Avenue, Lincolnwood, Illinois 60712

Ground Floor, 59 Gloucester Place, London W1U 8JJ
Customer Service: 1-800-595-8484 or customer_service@pilbooks.com

www.pilbooks.com

p i kids is a registered trademark of Publications International, Ltd.

ISBN-13: 978-1-4127-6241-0
ISBN-10: 1-4127-6241-3

Two Dalmatians named Pongo and Perdita lived happily in a London townhouse with their humans, Roger and Anita. Nanny lived with them and took care of them all.

Cooperation

Everyone needs help now and then. Cooperation means working together toward a common goal. When the Dalmatian puppies were in trouble, Pongo and Perdita couldn't rescue them alone. They barked for help! Dogs from all across the countryside worked together to save the puppies from Cruella De Vil.

Can you imagine how much cooperation you would need with one hundred and one Dalmatians living in *your* house?

The Twilight Bark reached an
old sheepdog far out
in the country.

The sheepdog heard puppies barking in the rundown De Vil mansion. He barked the news back to Pongo and Perdita.

Pongo and Perdita raced across the countryside to the mansion. They crept inside and found their puppies. All fifteen, plus dozens more. Ninety-nine spotted puppies! Cruella was planning to make a fur coat out of them!

Pongo and Perdita proceeded to teach the robbers a lesson.

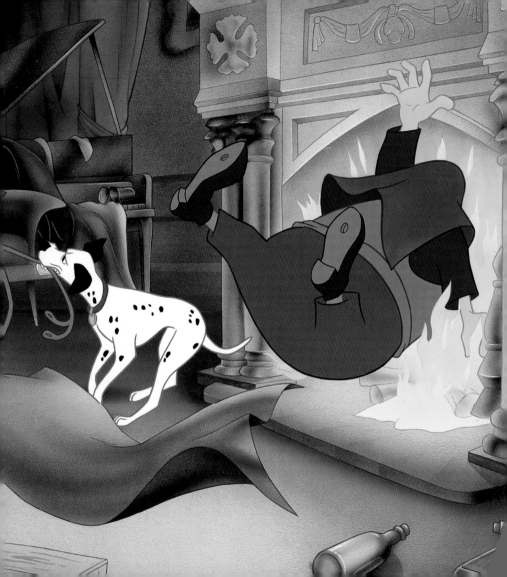

Pongo, Perdita, and the puppies helped each
other escape through a hole in the wall.
The robbers chased them, but they ran
to a blacksmith's shop, where a black
Labrador was waiting to help them.
There, the puppies all rolled
in some soot. They worked
together to cover their spots.
Now they looked like black
Labrador puppies! The soot-covered
puppies sneaked past Cruella and the
robbers, and crept into a waiting van.

Cruella saw the puppies getting into the van. But she wasn't looking for Labradors. Then snow washed one of the puppies clean. Spots! The puppies were Dalmatians!

"Get them!" cried Cruella.

The van sped off. The robbers chased it in their truck. Cruella chased it in her long car. Cruella drove so fast, she crashed into the robbers. The puppies sped off toward London.

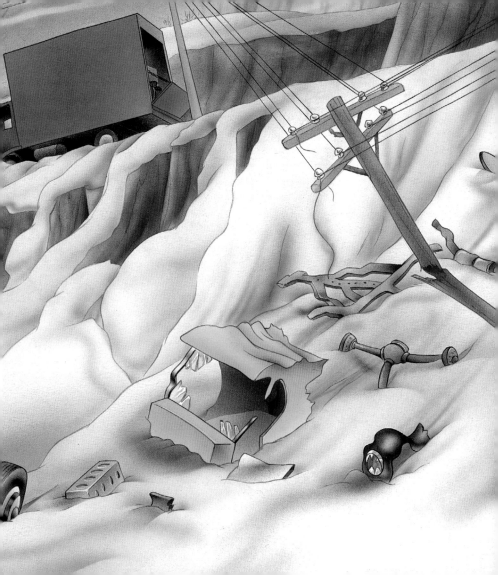

When Pongo, Perdita, and the puppies arrived home, Roger and Anita were delighted.

Nanny counted the puppies. "Ninety-nine," she said with a big smile. "Plus Pongo and Perdita. That's one hundred and one Dalmatians!"

Pongo and Perdita loved their big family. They knew they wouldn't have made it home without the cooperation of many of their friends. With the help of the Twilight Bark, the sheepdog in the country, and the Labrador, the puppies were rescued. They made it home because they all worked together.

When Pongo and Perdita arrived home, they were frantic. They searched everywhere for their puppies. They knew Cruella De Vil was to blame.

Finally Pongo said, "We can't do this alone. We need help!"

Pongo and Perdita began barking. Other dogs heard them and passed the Twilight Bark across the countryside.

Cruella De Vil was furious! "I'll be back!" she yelled. She stormed out, her fur coat sweeping around her.

Time passed, and the little puppies grew plump and happy.

Then one night, when the puppies were alone with Nanny, two strange-looking men came to the house. Nanny suspected they were up to no good, and sent them away. But later, they came back... and stole the puppies!

Cruella wanted to buy the puppies! Roger and Anita refused, of course!

"They are not for sale," Roger said.

One night, Pongo paced nervously. He was about to be a father. Perdita was having puppies.

Nanny counted the puppies. "Fifteen!" she cried.

Lightning flashed, and the door burst open with a *bang!* Cruella De Vil, Anita's old school friend, strode into the kitchen.